Double Duel

By Ace Landers
Illustrated by Dave White

SCHOLASTIC INC.

No part of this publication may be reproduced, stored in a
retrieval system, or transmitted in any form or by any means, electronic, mechanical,
photocopying, recording, or otherwise, without written permission of the copyright owner.
For information regarding permission, write to Scholastic Inc.,
Attention: Permissions Department, 557 Broadway, New York, NY 10012.

ISBN 978-0-545-46823-7

HOT WHEELS and associated trademarks and trade dress are owned by, and used under
license from Mattel. Inc. © 2013 Mattel, Inc. All Rights Reserved.

Published by Scholastic Inc. SCHOLASTIC and associated logos
are trademarks and/or registered trademarks of Scholastic Inc.

12 11 10 9 8 7 6   15 16 17 18/0

Printed in the U.S.A.   40
First printing, January 2013

Welcome to the top secret Hot Wheels Test Facility.

Today the drivers must complete the Double Loop racetrack.

They will race through a
hair-raising loop and jump
over the canyon.

Team Green is first to the starting line.

Team Blue wants in on the action, too.

The blue driver always prepares for a new stunt.

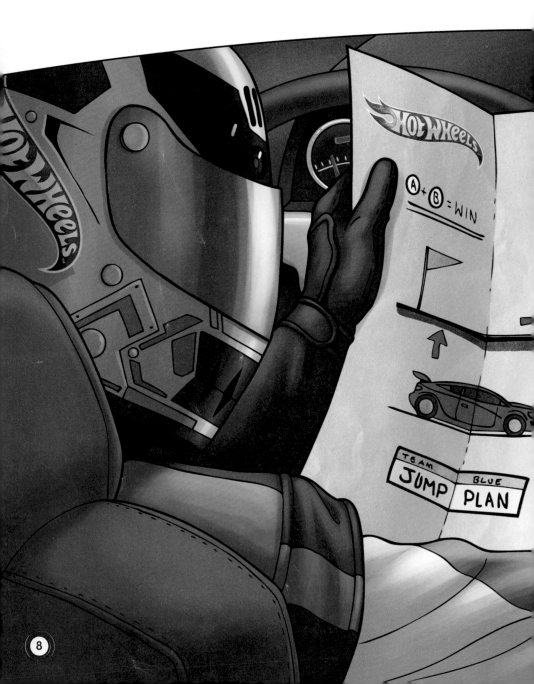

He wants to be perfect.

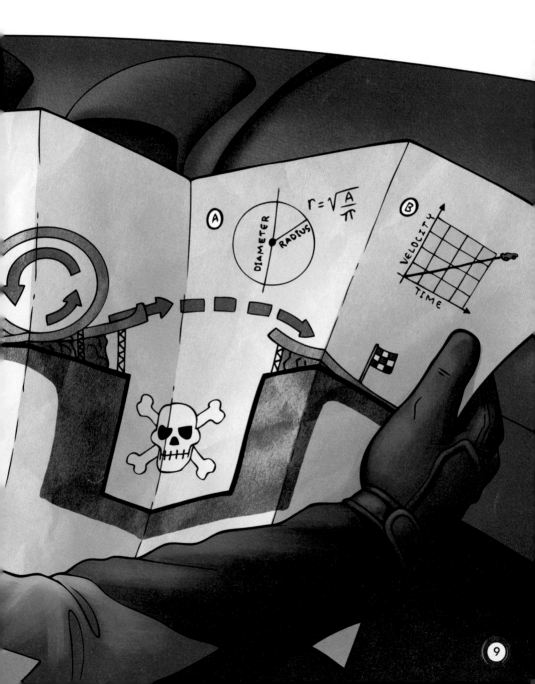

The green driver revs his engine. He is ready to go!

Finally, the blue driver is ready. The race can begin.

Both cars race up the track.
The green driver is faster.

The blue driver goes the right speed to make it around the loop.

The green driver is the
first up the loop.

But he is going too fast!
The green driver loses
control!

Watch out, Team Blue!

The green driver skids out and
misses the loop completely.

But the blue driver glides around the loop at the perfect speed.

TRACK 1

He hits the ramp and
launches into the air.

He flies over the canyon.

The blue driver lands safely!

But Team Green never gives up.

The green driver wants to try the stunt again.

This time he drives even faster.

But faster is not always better. The green driver skids out again!

The blue driver calls
the green driver over
his headset.

He tells the green driver his secret: Keep the exact same speed around the loop.

Now the green driver is ready to complete the Double Loop track.

The green driver zooms all the way around the loop this time.

Then he launches over the canyon!

He jumps farther than the blue driver!

When Team Hot Wheels works together, they cannot be beat!